TROLL STROLL

For everyone at Nosy Crow,
with huge scoopfuls of thanks – EW

For Ellie, Frankie & Jowan – DB

First published 2017 by Nosy Crow Ltd
The Crow's Nest, 10a Lant Street
London SE1 1QR
www.nosycrow.com

ISBN 978 0 85763 971 4 (HB)
ISBN 978 0 85763 972 1 (PB)

Nosy Crow and associated logos are trademarks
and/or registered trademarks of Nosy Crow Ltd

A CIP catalogue record for this book is available from the British Library.

Papers used by Nosy Crow are made from wood grown in sustainable forests.

Printed and bound in China by Imago

1 3 5 7 9 8 6 4 2 (HB)
1 3 5 7 9 8 6 4 2 (PB)

Elli Woollard   David Barrow

TROLL STROLL

This is the Troll

and his big bowl of food,

the goats that he's guzzled,

the bones that he's chewed.

And this is the Troll with his big empty bowl,
who's fed up with goats and so goes for a stroll –
down the steep hill and then **over** a ridge,
who **stomps** through the town and then stops at a bridge.

Here on the bridge is the boy that he spied,
pedalling along for a nice pleasant ride.

"Mmm," says the Troll. "There is **nothing** I like
quite as much as a nice juicy **boy** on his **bike.**

A guzzle!

A gollop!

Who wants to eat goats?

I'll **chomp** little children and **chew** up their coats."

"Stop!" cries the boy. "Please don't eat me just yet!
There is something much better behind me, I bet!
I'm titchy-tiny, but **look** at that **car!**
There are **four** children in there, much **fatter** by far."

"Huh!" grunts the Troll. "I suppose you are right. I will **gulp** them all up in one **gobblesome** bite."

Here right behind him the **car** is now coming.

It reaches the bridge with a rattling and humming.

"**Yum**," says the Troll. "I adore lovely **meals**

when they're still piping **hot** and delivered on **wheels**.

A guzzle!

A gollop!

Who wants to eat goats?

I'll **chomp** little children and **chew** up their coats."

EWDB1

"**Stop!**" cries the driver. "Don't eat us just yet!
There is something much better behind us, I bet!
We're only teeny, but **look** behind us,
there are **plenty** of children to chew on that **bus.**"

"Huh!" grunts the Troll. "I suppose you are right. I will **gulp** them all up in one **gobblesome** bite."

Here is the **bus** as it **races** along
with a class full of children all singing a song.

"Yum," says the Troll. "Little **snacks** make me drool
when they're all stuck together
and **flavoured** with **school**.

A guzzle! A gollop!

Who wants to eat goats?

I'll **chomp** little children and **chew** up their coats."

This is the Troll who's now **licking** his lips.

"These children," he growls, "would be **tasty** with **chips.**"

But, **"Stop!"** cry the children.

"There's something much **bigger!**"

And then right behind them there comes . . .

. . . a huge digger!

"Yum," says the Troll. "Oh, what slobbersome luck!
Such **scrumptious** young morsels,
all covered in **muck**!

A guzzle!
A gollop!
Who wants to eat goats?
I'll **chomp** little children and **chew** up their coats.

You're better by **far** than the
Billy Goats Gruff!"
And he **grabs** at the children,
but not fast enough . . .

"Yum!" say the children. "Oh, what a delight!
We will **guzzle** you up in one **gobblesome** bite."

They lift up the Troll in the air with their scoop,

and they yell, "Now it's

teatime!

Let's make some . . .

Troll soup!"

This is the Troll feeling really quite small,
who thinks that a goat might taste good after all . . .

And this is the Troll
running **fast** as can be,
as he races back home . . .

. . . to eat **goat** for his tea.